HOOTS & TOOTS & HAIRY BRUTES

Books by Larry Shles
Moths & Mothers, Feathers & Fathers
Hoots & Toots & Hairy Brutes

HOOTS & TOOTS & HAIRY BRUTES

The Continuing Adventures of Squib

Written and illustrated by
Larry Shles

Houghton Mifflin Company Boston 1985

Library of Congress Cataloging-in-Publication Data

Shles, Larry.
Hoots & toots & hairy brutes.

Summary: Troubled because he can only toot and not
hoot like other owls, Squib finally learns that
it is how one uses one's individual talents that makes
the difference.
[1. Fables.   2. Owls—Fiction.   3. Self-acceptance—
Fiction]   I. Title.   II. Title: Hoots and toots and hairy brutes.
PZ8.2.S44HO   1985   [Fic]   85-13995
ISBN 0-395-36556-2
ISBN 0-395-39503-8 (pbk.)

Printed in the United States of America

Cloth   P Pbk.   AL 10 9 8 7 6 5 4 3 2 1

To my daughter, Stacy, with much love
To Mahala Cox, whose elegant vision enriches the world
To Terry Cain, for invaluable guidance and faith

HOOTS & TOOTS & HAIRY BRUTES

Squib was an unusually tiny owl

who couldn't hoot or fly.

Because of his problems, every owl ignored him.
Every day when he came home from his adventures,
Squib was eager to tell his parents about the amazing
things he'd seen.

"Mommy, you'll never guess what I saw this morning," Squib would toot. "I saw the strangest ants. They were carrying . . ."

"Hoot up, dear, I can hardly hear you," his mother would say.

Squib knew she wasn't really listening, but he tried again in his loudest toot. "I saw these weird ants . . ."

"I'm glad you did, dear," his mother would say as she continued with her chores.

Squib fared no better when he
went out to play with the other
young owls. The only time they let
Squib join in was when they
played owlpile.
Squib always wound up at the
bottom of the heap.

Nor would the owls make room for Squib around the campfire. Instead he would have to listen to their horror stories from the chilly shadows.

In these stories they whispered of the ugly and evil Hairy Brute and how he terrorized the forest. Without warning, loud explosions erupted from a stick he carried. Hundreds of forest animals had been injured or killed by the Brute.

"I know about the Hairy Brute, too," Squib tooted. But his tiny voice was swallowed by the darkness and the crackling of the fire.

Squib had already learned much about the Hairy Brute from his parents.

"He is so hideous, Squib," they would tell him. "He kills for no reason. You must always keep a keen eye out for him. And should you ever spot him, remain absolutely motionless and make no sound."

Squib began waking up in the middle of the night with terrible visions of the Brute.

One morning Squib was awakened by a sharp explosion and the frantic hoots of his neighbors. The Brute had attacked a young owl in the next tree. Now no place in the forest was safe from the ravages of the fiendish Brute.

But as Squib drew nearer to hear more, the adult owls fell silent and moved away.

Denied any real details, Squib began painting pictures in his mind of what such a terrible monster might look like.

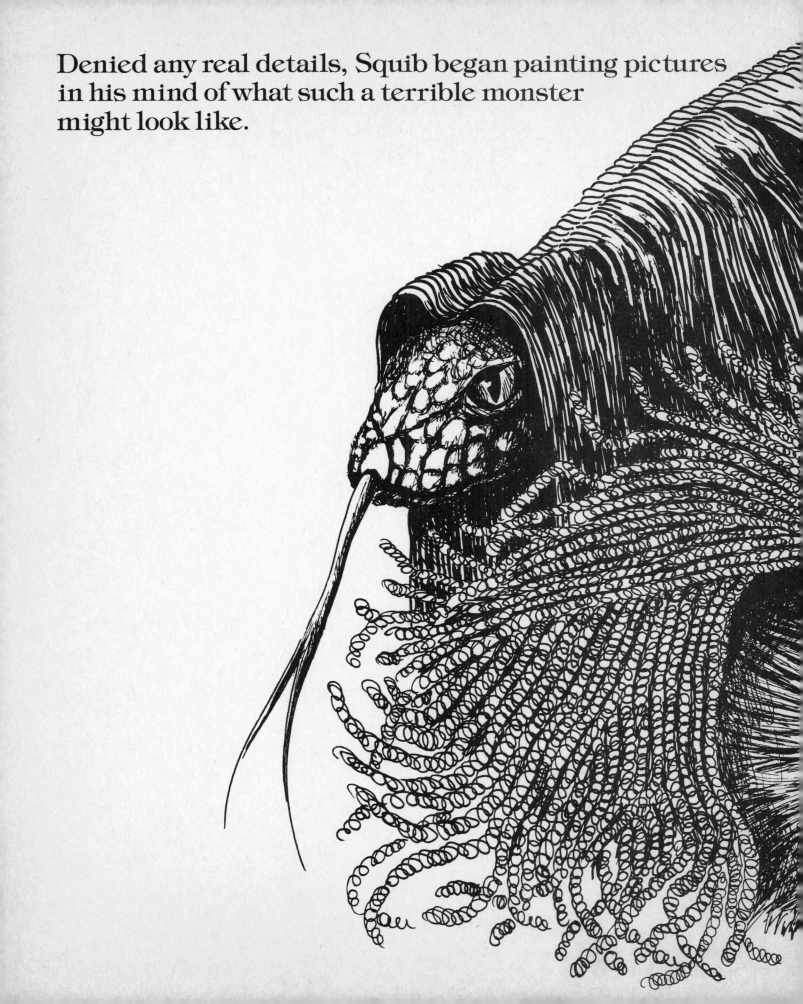

If only *I* were the Hairy Brute, Squib thought. I would be big, powerful, and feared. No one could ignore me then!

Half convinced that he *was* the Hairy Brute, Squib bombarded his elders with questions.

"Is the Brute a huge furry frog? Why can't he stay in his own forest? Dad, could you beat him up if he came to *our* nest?"

"Squib, when you're old enough to hoot, you'll be ready to understand such things," an adult would reply. "In the meantime, just hop off and play by yourself."

This attitude made Squib feel tinier than the tiny owl he already was.

After much thought, he came upon a solution to his problem. Since he could never be scary like the Brute, he'd have to learn how to hoot.

And when his toot became a hoot, everyone would listen to him.

Squib began practicing. He puffed out his chest,
thought HOOT!, and let it rip.
But it would come out as only a trivial *toot*.

toot

Squib tried to hoot on snoots and boots. He tried to hoot on fruits and newts. He even imagined hooting on the top of Hairy Brutes.

But all that ever came out was his weak,
>   pathetic
>   *toot.*

If only he could hoot like his father! When Dad lost his temper, he alerted the forest for miles around.

Inspired, Squib went off to practice
again. He took a deep breath, thought of
his father's hoot, and tore loose. *"Toot."*
Now there was a sound that would
terrorize even the Hairy Brute! Or so
Squib thought. Everyone else just
thought he was going nuts.

The harder he tried, the more surprising the results became. Squib's *toots* were turning into *moos, oinks, caws, snorts, ribbits, peeps,* and *neighs.*

Embarrassed, he'd look around, hoping no one had heard him.

Deciding he just didn't give a hoot, Squib turned into a pest. He snuck up on a sleeping cat, perched on his ear, and unleashed his mightiest *toot*. The cat didn't even open an eye.

He crept up on a blue jay, perched on a branch, and let out a sudden *toot*. The blue jay, irritated, unleashed a screech that blasted Squib off the branch.

Totally dejected, Squib went to his mother. "I want to be able to hoot, Mom," he said in a very whiny *toot*.

His mother, seeing how miserable Squib was, made appointments with experts to determine why he was hootless.

The orthodontist was certain that Squib's problem was the result of overbeak. Squib was fitted for braces and headgear.

Once the braces were removed, Squib again tried to hoot. Concentrating on changing the "t" sound to an "h" sound, he mumbled his new word. It was strange. The "t" and "h" had now merged. Squib's first sound after his braces came off was *"thooth."*

Next Squib's mother took him to a psychowlogist.
"This youngster is too tense to hoot," he exclaimed.
Squib was instructed to breathe deeply and repeat the
sound "Owlmmmmmmm" over and over again.

Squib formed his relaxed beak into an "oo" shape
and calmly breathed out the sound he hoped would be
his first hoot.

Well, it wasn't. And it wasn't a toot, either.
His new sound was *shoosh.* Squib was
too relaxed now to even give a toot.

As a last resort, Squib's mother hired a tutor to teach him. At first Squib was confused. He could already toot. Why did he need a tooter? And if a tutor taught hooting, certainly she should be called a hooter rather than a tooter.

Once this confusion was settled, Squib's hoot tutor, who was cuter and astuter than most hooters, launched him into his lessons. Squib was instructed to practice all his "h" sounds:

ho-ho-he-he-hi-hi-huh-huh-ha-ha-ha-ha.........hah! The hoot tutor called Squib's family together to hear her student's progress. All eyes were on Squib as he was placed center branch. Clearing his throat and looking skyward, he meekly brought forth his new sound.

Before he could even hear what he had said, all his
relatives were laughing. Squib spoke again.
The laughter was louder. And no wonder.
Froot was his new sound. *"Froot"*?
The tutor had done nothing more than
turn Squib into a frooty tutee.

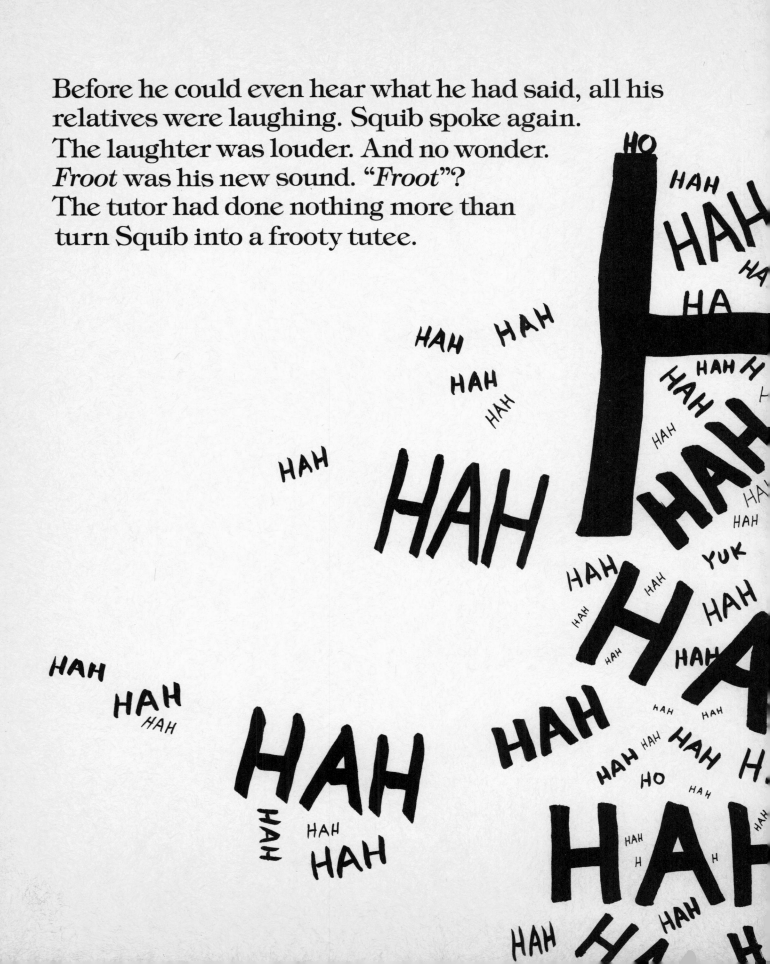

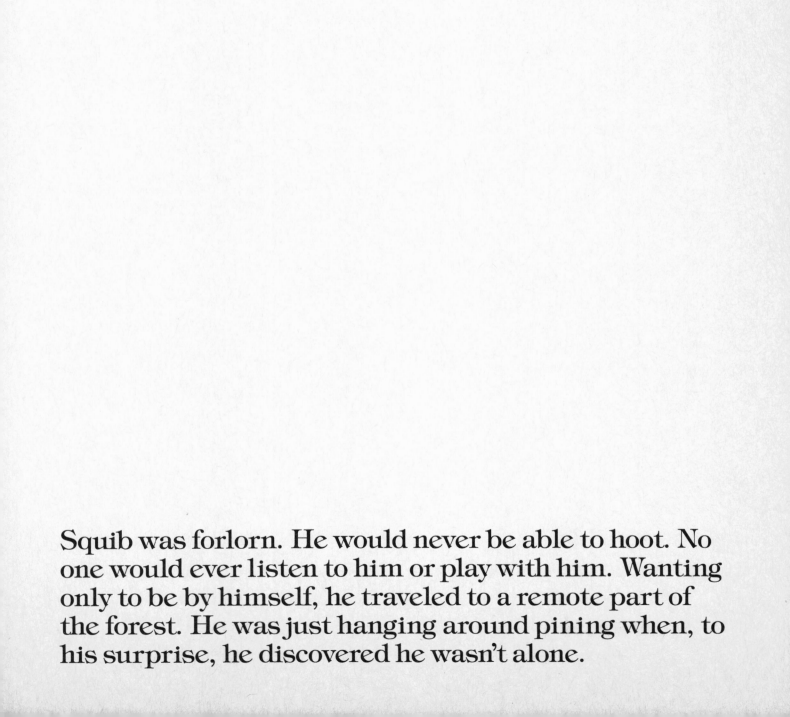

Squib was forlorn. He would never be able to hoot. No one would ever listen to him or play with him. Wanting only to be by himself, he traveled to a remote part of the forest. He was just hanging around pining when, to his surprise, he discovered he wasn't alone.

He had accidentally journeyed to the place where his parents were hunting for the day's meal. How regal and powerful they looked as they scanned the distant meadow for field mice.

 Suddenly Squib saw the terrible beast.

The gigantic creature had loomed up just a short distance from him. It was the Hairy Brute. He was poised, staring at Squib's mother and father, and pointing an ugly-looking stick at them.

Squib realized the lives of his parents were at stake. His heart began to pound; his wing tips went stiff; his toes curled up from fright. He had to warn them immediately, but he knew the only thing they could hear at that distance would be a mighty hoot.

Please, God, let this be a hoot. Please!

Squib concentrated as hard as he could, opened his tiny beak wide, and let out his warning.......

"Toot!"

.......It was still a toot—but the most remarkable toot you'd ever want to hear. It wasn't loud, but it was crystal clear and pure.

Like a swift arrow, Squib's toot flew across the meadow, alerting his parents. Startled to hear such a beautiful sound, they looked around and discovered the Hairy Brute. Instantly they flew off the branch. The Brute's shot rang out. Too late! Squib's parents had soared to safety.

From that moment on, Squib found that his life was changed. All his struggle and practice trying to hoot had created a toot that was unique. And once he realized the value of his tiny yet beautiful toot, Squib stood prouder. The young owls now invited him to join in all their games. And when they played owlpile, Squib would wind up on the top of the heap.

Now when Squib tooted around a sleeping cat, cats from all over the neighborhood would awaken.

They would converse

with him for hours about their   day's adventures.

Within the campfire circle, Squib now had his own Hairy Brute story to tell. Everyone listened intently and asked him many questions when he finished.

Squib now knew that his toot could be worth as much as any hoot in the world.

11048085
ISBN 0-395-39503-8